Daughter of the Night

Daughter of the Night

RICHARD S. SHAVER

ÆGYPAN PRESS

From *Amazing Stories*, December, 1948.

Special thanks to Greg Weeks, Mary Meehan, and the Online Distributed Proofreading Team (which can be found at http://www.pgdp.net).

Daughter of the Night
A publication of
ÆGYPAN PRESS

www.aegypan.com

The evil magic of the Goddess Diana turned men to stone. Would the power of the strange Eos be strong enough to turn them back to living men?

Chapter I

Like a flash of light the gleaming sword swept down. A fraction of a second later a portion of it no longer gleamed: it was crimson! And Queen Dionaea's head bounced down the stairway into her garden of live oaks. A few seconds of thought remained to it before it would be very dead; but her thought was confused by shock – her eyes rolled uncontrollably while she tried to remember some cantrap or rune from her long association with the Goddess Diana. Desperately she tried to recite the proper abracadabra to stay the swift death that was sweeping through her mind; but it is hard for a head to chant a charm with no body to draw a breath. . . .

Druga, his job of execution finished, sheathed his bloody sword and turning, stalked away. Thus it was that he did not see the amazing thing that happened in the gloom of the ancient live oaks. . . .

Baena was a serpent, a huge river of strength up to his giant head, and he lived among the mighty branches of the oaks. Being a serpent, Baena was far from equal to a human being in his brainpower, but even his dim perception told him that harm had come to his one and only benefactress – and that meant harm to him, too, for Queen Dionaea had always cared for the needs of his stomach. Through her he ate and lived. Without her, he would die. And so, he glided rapidly down from the trunk of his favorite tree and emerged into the paths of the garden just as Dionaea's bleeding head rolled out from the base of the steps.

Baena coiled his length protectingly about Dionaea. For an instant he was at a loss, noting her horribly desperate attempts to speak without breath, her mouth opening and closing and her tongue licking snakelike in and out.

Baena realized after a moment that there was no hope for the Queen to go on living. A head must have a body.

Glancing about, Baena saw nothing but the numerous coils of *his own body,* and after an instant's hesitation, he took his tail in his mouth up to the tenth joint and bit it off! Shrinking along all his length with the terrible necessity that faced him, Baena quickly slapped the bloody stump of his tail fast to the bleeding neck of Dionaea and said one of the few magic spells he could remember. . . .

Turning his body slowly until his severed nerves told his spine that the connections were as accurate as could be expected, Baena waited while the spell slowly took effect. He lay there all night, waiting for his own life's blood to reanimate the mind of Dionaea.

As Dionaea came back to her senses, Baena began to experience the strange phenomena of wanting to go two ways at once, and as the phenomena became more and more troublesome, he decided that he had better have an understanding with Dionaea once and for all.

But what poor male ever won an argument with a woman?

Thus it was that Baena resigned himself to a life of traveling backward, and that was that.

As a snake, he wished only to eat and bask in his favorite tree, but as Dionaea, he wanted only one thing – and that with all the fervor of hate a sorceress is capable of – a fitting revenge on the man who had visited her execution upon her!

Day and night Dionaea plotted, and in her mind a fitting revenge grew – it would include the lovely Feronia, Druga's beloved. . . . Carefully she prepared the incantation.

It is here that my story really begins. What has happened, and how it happened is of little consequence to what is to come – except perhaps to introduce you to the characters. It is very simple. Dionaea was a very evil sorceress, and Druga, most heroic of men, had long sought to bring her into his power, and to end her evil days. Armed with the white magic of Feronia, his loved one, who was also a sorceress, but one who worked her charms only for the good of mankind, he had tracked Dionaea to her castle, and there slain her. Or he would have, had it not been for Baena, the serpent. . . .

What is past is past. It is best not to think of it. There is much in the past of all of us that would need a long, tiresome explanation to a newcomer, and you are newcomers. To explain all of the past to everyone would be an impossible task. You need know only that Druga, champion of mankind, and his lovely Feronia, face now the most awful menace of their lives, and unknowing of it, too, for thinking their arch enemy slain!

Where do all our characters live? In Fantasia, a land far away. A land where wondrous things always happen. It is of one of the most wondrous adventures of all that you are about to hear now – let the past lie, cold and dead as it is, and come with me into the present, and into *danger!*

Who am I? Does it make any difference? If you must know, I am the Red Dwarf, and I have seen and recorded *everything!* I was there, and if you can but understand, everything has happened *because* I was there! If it were not so, how could you be sure what I tell is true? For it *is* true. . . .

It was evening. As Druga and Feronia sat talking, before retiring, the horror fell upon them.

Feronia's hair fell like a living torrent to fondle her gleaming shoulders and toy everywhere with the strangely electric invisible vitality of her glowing skin. Her eyes were molten pools, dark and liquid as the waters of the lost caverns, and the brows above them were mystic lines of beauty left by the touch of a raven wing. Her generous mouth was smiling the wondrous lovely magic that was Feronia, red as a newborn rose, dewy and waiting for Druga. Her capable hands were soft with expecting him, and cooler than the moss beneath the fern.

Her breasts were as naked as sun-bleached coral, white as a cloud in a summer sky, white as truth, white as her own teeth laughing tantalizingly at him.

Quite suddenly, shockingly, her lovely figure became transfused with a vile, interloping energy that struck at Druga's sensitivities with a sickening piercingness, so that he sprang to his feet in fear.

Standing there helplessly, Druga watched the evil energy transform the strong, deep breasted beauty of his Feronia, change her devilishly and subtly and gradually before his suffering eyes.

The white magic of her body became transfused with dark, throbbing force, and as she strove to rise and act, Druga saw that she could not move her limbs in any way!

Before his eyes her skin turned black as ebony, her eyes became stony and fixed; even the sweet curling of her hair became hard and solid, her whole body became changed to black, hated stone.

As suddenly as the horrible pulsing had come, it went away, leaving Druga that least of all desirable women, one of virtuous stone.

So with one stroke Dionaea repaid Druga and Feronia; Druga by the loss of his best beloved, and Feronia by the retention of her faculties in a body of stone. That Feronia had to sit immovable and watch poor Druga in his grief and loss was particularly excruciating.

Days of horror dragged by.

No matter what he proposed to do upon arising, mid-morning found him reclining before the frozen statuelike body of his beloved, and night would come down at last to hide the black stone of Feronia from his wet eyes.

This existence became at last unbearable, and he resolved to go out into the world and seek some means of making his days less horrible to him. That Feronia was not dead, and that he might have obtained her release by appealing to some greater power, did not occur to Druga in his grief. Indeed he could never become accustomed to the ways of witches and their overlords, nor to thinking in terms of magic at all. He was a logical person, and no matter what wonders he blundered into and saw with his own eyes, he never quite believed any of it.

It was with a heavy heart that Druga sealed up the doors of Feronia's home and made his sad way to the stable, mounted and rode slowly away.

All night he rode, not choosing his way, but letting the horse do the thinking, and in the warm sun of late morning lay down to sleep where the horse had led him.

As the days passed in heedless wandering, the deep hurt of his loss lessened, and he began to take note of the road that led ever on and on to he knew not what, except that it beckoned, as paths and highways alike have a way of doing to the traveler.

As his spirits became lighter, he began to take stock of the country through which he passed, and to note all the strange and curious things that hovered always just outside normal vision. They were not hidden from Druga, who had more than ordinary vision, one of Feronia's witch gifts to him, and many a strange fact of life he picked up from the circumambient apparent emptiness.

It was with this far-seeing sense that Druga now noticed a glowing, golden vibrance spreading an invisible, but terrifically felt glory, all across the northern horizon. He turned the horse's head toward that glory, no more able to avoid the decision than is a moth the flame.

What it was that he sensed he did not surely know, but his memory supplied him with vague and haunting clues which he could not quite drag out into the light of reason. It did not stand to reason, but there it was ahead, the lure of woman augmented by some magic into a glory visible as sunlight, strong as some great whirlpool of energy, drawing him resistlessly on and on.

Many a mile later, Druga came to a point where he could see with his eyes on ahead and into the shining core of that field of golden vibrance.

"One of the universal poles of life!" cried Druga. In his studies Druga had learned that just as the world has a North and South magnetic pole, so does the universe have opposite poles of life-magnetic-energy. One of these is female, and inducts in all life a female nature; the other is male and inducts in all life a male nature, just as the North and South pole induct in all iron and in kindred matter a North and South magnetic pole.

"It is no wonder it draws me, it is the force which makes all life attractive to all other life. . . ."

Druga knew that there was no use his trying to resist the attraction anymore than a compass could resist pointing north. So he rode onward into the glory, musing that it was strange this universal pole of infinite space should, in its drifting, have crossed his own path upon this planet.

As he neared the center of the increasing ecstasy, Druga's mind and body became cleaned of all desires but one, and that was to reach the exact center and there remain. Along with others, his affection for Feronia was burned away, leaving him helpless in the grip of this emotion greater by far than any other.

Glory, golden ecstatic glory, poured through him in a titanic flood, and nearer and nearer he came to the shining central core of the mighty field of universal energy.

As he came at last to clear vision of the core, he saw floating there a vast, circular disk of golden hue, and upon the disk a tremendous mansion. Beneath the disk was only the shining golden air, and it came to Druga that this mansion must be a singularly pleasant place to live. He cast about for some means of lifting himself across the space of nothingness that separated the dull earth and the shining plane of the disk. So near to the delightful power that drew, and yet so impossible to get nearer because of the nothingness between him and the disk, Druga at last rode on beneath and on to the very center of the shining darkness beneath the great disk.

Now he was truly at the pole and dynamic source of female magnetic attraction! Shaking in every fiber with the blasting force of the terrific center of this universal power, Druga stood, a moth caught up in a whirlpool too great to understand or withstand; and he would have died there after a time, unable to move from the spot.

But overhead the great disk suddenly showed a light, a beam of ruby red that laddered down to him through the golden murk of energy, and above that beam of ruby light he made out a shining form that beckoned to him. Trying to answer the invitation, Druga put out a hand to the red beacon and found it solid to his touch, a rod of crystal, thick as a man's body and with hand-holds and foot-steps hewn into it. He got off the horse and ascended the weird ladder toward the shining being who beckoned.

A woman divinely tall and with hair like ripened wheat, modeled of hammered sunlight, her glowing flesh surcharged with the infinite female energies of the Universal Pole, met him at the topmost step of the ladder.

He stepped out into the halls of the mansion by her side, unable to speak with the ecstasy that poured from her. For such was the nature of that disk, that it concentrated the magnetic flow of the Pole field so that it emanated solely from the body of this woman.

She drew a robe of the purest blue about her glowing body, to insulate and screen off the terrific irresistible force. His mind speculated constantly and intriguingly on what would happen to him if she should desire him and cast off this protective robe?

So thinking, Druga walked beside her vital beauty, noting the deep lagoons of her eyes upon him, curious, blue as the sea, shaded by long lashes of dusky amber shielding from him some deep wisdom that she must keep from him just yet. Try as he might he could not plumb the swirling depths within her mind. Reach as he would he could find there nothing to read but pictured vastnesses of strange beauty and violent passions strongly withheld, nooks and crannies of mysterious, unreadable thought far beyond his understanding to interpret. His senses turned away from the inner mysterious glory of her mind, and his eyes came to rest on her lips, crimson arches riper than tropic flowers, moist as with desire, wide and capable and smiling upon him with a woman's will to captivate twinkling all along the crimson outline of her smile. Behind her lips her teeth gleamed, almost avid, parted in a hunger that he did not then care to understand. Her breasts were ripe and full, beneath the blue, shielding robe, her waist a column of cunningly tapered ivory rounding into hips and thighs of masterful curves, moving with mysterious woman magic beneath the vaguely transparent shimmer of her robe.

Druga stared into the blue lagoons of her eyes, and at last asked what was closest to his heart.

"Who and what are you, who lives here at the summit of female attraction in all the universe?"

"In ancient times, many were the men who were alive enough to sense this pole and come questing to me as the moth to the flame. But in these times, who are you to sense the mighty energy of the Universal Pole and be drawn here to me?"

"I am Druga, and I am sad and bereft, and I wander seeking death as much as life. If the name tells you anything, you are welcome to the information. I am no immortal. Are you then one of those who do not die?"

"I have been called by many names in the past, but men sometimes remember me as Aurora. Others have called me Eos."

"A fool is easily convinced, immortal Eos. But though I have not lived long, I have learned that appearances are deceiving and not to be trusted. How do I know that I am not out of my mind, and this place and yourself but delusions?"

"You *are* in a state, aren't you? You must tell me all about it; there will be plenty of time. For there is no way for a man to leave here of his own will."

"What became of all those visitors you tell me came here in the old time?"

Eos laughed loudly, a clear ringing laugh.

"Perhaps you had better worry about that, Druga! What do you suppose could have happened to them?"

Chapter II

Eos led him into a great feasting chamber, and Druga saw there a great host of men sitting, as to a feast, side by side.

Each one of them was of solid black stone. The fact struck Druga's mind with a terrible impact. With a face like thunder he said:

"So it was you who turned my Feronia to stone, to drag me here to you by your spells, and then when you tire of me to turn me likewise into stone?"

The woman recoiled from his murderous rage, crying out in a shocked voice, a voice of virtue unjustly accused:

"Surely you don't think that I had anything to do with this? These men are the curse an enemy has put upon me; and every creature that I ever loved she has turned into stone soon or late and left me here alone forever. There is no cruelty like the cruelty of Diana Triformis."

The rage passed slowly from Druga, and left him weak and glad that his hands had not found their way to that glorious throat, as they had seemed about to do. For here was a woman who had suffered the same loss as he.

"Eos, we must take thought together, for it seems we have a common enemy. My own Feronia, a woman such as was only created by the Gods once in all Time, was turned into similar black stone before my eyes not long ago. We have a common enemy, and we must find a remedy for this curse she puts upon us. Else I will go through life as you have gone, with everything pleasant removed from it."

The artful eyes of Eos softened, and that mystery living in their depths lightened, her arms became soft pillars of the temple of her beauty as she lowered herself into the big chair at the head of that gloomy feasting board of death. Druga picked up the big body of one of the stone figures, carried it lightly to the side of the hall, and set it there on a bench. Then he took the vacant place at the board beside the queen of the palace of the dead.

Druga related to Eos all the events that had transpired since the lopping off of Dionaea's head. She surmised, as did he, that this deed was the one that had led Diana to turn the spell of the black stone loose upon Druga as upon Eos.

"There must be found a way of turning the spells of this Goddess into harmless attempts," said Druga. "We cannot sit here and wait for her cruelty to work us greater harm. What can we do?"

"I have had long long years to plan a revenge upon her, but nothing I have been able to do has had any effect," Eos said.

The desire that Druga could no more help than he could help breathing, looking upon the pole of all desire that shone its energies through the flesh of Eos, now spoke, and Druga said with a tongue that was thick:

"Then, Eos, the very next time that Diana happens to think of you, I too will become stone, and if we are to have joy of each other, we had better have it soon, before I become as these others you have loved."

Eos looked at him sadly, her lips glistening with an unearthly dew and her eyes shining like chained lightnings.

"It was that thought that betrayed me every time, Druga. Each of those men said much those same words to me when he learned the fate that awaited him, and for each of them my heart turned to water and we spent our time in dalliance instead of spending our energies trying to overcome the work of my enemy.

"For each of them I tried to give all there was of pleasure while they yet had breath, as one tries to give water to a man about to die of fever. I was only that much more hurt by their death – for such giving of the self opens one to the deepest pangs of parting.

"That is the agony Diana designed for me, and she has done this to me since that time I brought a young man to her island that was sacred to her only. This time, Druga, there will be none of that for us; we will try some other medicine than love for each other against this evil. Work, we will try!"

"There speaks my dead Feronia," murmured Druga, sadly. And for thought of her he forgot to feel the denial of his desire for the body of this woman, a body filled with the energies of the whole Universal Pole of female magnetism. That he should lose that glory was nothing beside the pang he felt at thought of Feronia; and the wise Eos smiled to note that this man had not forgotten his love even in the face of her infinite attraction.

"If we went back to Feronia's home, might it not be that her work would give you some inkling of how Diana might be overcome?" Druga was thoughtful.

"I can only try," Eos answered him. "We will go there. I will examine her work and her notes, and you will show me her laboratories that I have heard of even here. Together, we might get an answer."

Eos got up from the board, and went to a small chamber at the edge of the disk. There her hands sent the disk slanting upward into the sky. As they left the center of the pole of animal magnetism, Eos' body and face changed subtly. Druga was released from the power of the pole's attraction, and whether that was a good thing or not he could not say, except that every atom of his body wanted to return there to that place and remain.

"How is it, Eos, that the pole does not repel your female nature as it attracts the male? Would it not repel an ordinary woman so that she could not approach it?"

"In that you are wrong, Druga. The nature of this life-energy is not the same as ordinary iron magnetism. Like poles do not repel, but are unaffected. It is in fact only invigorating to me, making me stronger. So it would be if you were at the other end of the universe. At the male pole you would be vastly invigorated, not repelled. Do you understand?"

"It is only sad that the poles lie at opposite ends of the universe," murmured Druga, looking askance at Eos.

"Whatever might you be thinking, Druga? If such power arced between man and woman they would be consumed!"

"But what a death, what a death," murmured Druga. Her sudden laughter rang through the hall of death incongruously, and at the sound they fell silent again and did not speak for thinking of the corpses waiting there for what would never come.

"How many men has Diana and her friends killed through the years? Enough to populate a couple of planets, I should say?"

"Diana? With her bow and arrows alone she used to account for a good many; and later, as she learned more evil arts, there was no record kept. She has been a most evil goddess, yet men worship her."

"Why? A goddess that kills a man for seeing her is a fiend! And her maidens may not see a man, either. It is a strange life she leads, for a true woman. She must be other than female."

"That could be, Druga," murmured Eos.

The morning sun glittered from the streams and from the little glass foot-bridge that shimmered magically across and up in a great arc to the door in the side of the cliff. Eos sighed at the beauty.

"This wife of yours was a housekeeper, I note, with an eye for art."

"Her art and her work were always first, Eos. She was an uncommon hard woman to get used to, but she made a man of me."

"That I can see," agreed Eos, and Druga looked at her twice to know what she meant. "You owe everything to Feronia, according to you, and nothing to yourself."

"Very little, Goddess. But I do not exaggerate, she was. . . ."

"Well, never mind it now. I grow weary of Feronia this and Feronia that. I will judge for myself whether she understood you or no."

"She was extremely understanding," said Druga.

Days passed, and much hard work, Eos studying the laboratory notes of Feronia, and Druga himself reading them over and trying to think of some way he himself might strike back at their mutual enemy.

"Nothing that she has developed can be used directly against Diana without her surviving to fight back. This would have been fatal to Dionaea, but after all, as you have said – she is dead."

"She ought to be dead, I cut her head off!"

"That usually does the trick."

They decided to leave the laboratory the next morning, and that evening Druga picked up the stone statue of his Feronia and carried it carefully aboard the disk, placing her there – one woman among the thousand-odd dead heroes of the long dead past. Druga sadly made a place for her at the head of the board. He did not think of it, but Feronia now sat where Eos herself had spent many a sad hour, sitting and gazing at her dead lovers.

With the stone Feronia gone, the vast and multiplex-walled chambers of mystery and magic assumed a new atmosphere, and Druga found himself talking to Eos that night as if he was not a man whose heart was dead.

She sat in the place from which he had removed the black stone body of Feronia, and Druga could not help but compare the glowing life of her with the dead thing that had sat there.

The hammered sunlight of her hair made curls and waves of beauty about the white shores of her shoulders. She had let the robe of insulative blue drop from her, exposing the very heart of her beauty he had feared to see when she was herself filled with the flow of the Pole of Life Energy. And Druga wondered a little whether she were not still somehow the center and pivot of the energy, for his senses reeled with looking, and his will crumbled into forgotten ashes. He sank to the silken couch beside her, and his eyes burned with flashing energies like meteors plunging into the Northern lights.

Eos held her breath, and her eyes burned into his with greater and greater force, for she had been dreaming and weeping and waiting there at the Pole-of-all-Life for so many cold empty years – waiting for the curse to be lifted so that she could begin to live again.

With the last shred of her own will Eos murmured: "Let us go into the disk and leave at once for Armora, and think no more of each other or surely we will sink into the raptures we desire and forget to fight. Then I will awake and find you too turned into stone, and myself again alone against her. I have been unable to fight alone."

"If that is your will, do not fail to shield your beauty with that robe you wear. For I cannot resist the power in your loveliness anymore than a straw in the wind!"

Eos closed the robe against his gaze, and like two people weighted down with lead in every limb, they got up and went out of the darkened chambers, and Druga closed the great doors and locked them. Silently, not touching each other, they walked down the bridge of glass.

They entered the mansion on the disk, and Eos sent it sharply upward. There was blood on her lower lip where she had bit it, and Druga's nails had bitten into his palms.

Druga noted that the great golden glow in the sky had approached near to the valley that Feronia had made her home, and he said:

"This pole of life seems to follow you about! Is there some relation between you and it, so that you cannot be apart?"

Eos looked at him, smiling sadly, her eyes far-off with other thoughts.

"I have been taught, in the far past, that there was a Mother of Life, a real woman, mighty and majestic beyond thinking, who lived there at the pole and ordered life to be as it should be. That she is my ancestor, and that there is some relation between the life energies and myself, may be true, Druga. Whether the pole follows me, or whether coincidence is governed by some magic so that we are never far apart, I know not. Knowledge is a thing now lost from life, as we know it, Druga. We can only guess at these truths, and never learn them surely."

"Now you are not telling me all you know, Eos."

"I would not tell you what I only guess, Druga. And I do not surely know anything, anymore. I have spent so much time brooding and alone."

"Forgive me, Eos. An eagle cannot fly with crows, and I will never again put myself forward. When you have need of me, I will be here, and when you need only your own thoughts, why then go apart; I will not seek you out. I forget who and what you are, for my senses are strained beyond endurance with the power of you."

"You are no crow, Druga. But in me is an adult mind, and you are as a child, whom I must teach and raise up gradually to my estate. Every parent grows impatient of ignorance in their offspring. One day, if time keeps treading the self-same mill, we will be crushed together like grapes and pressed clean. Until then, be my knight, and think not of me, except with pity for the broken heart that beats inside me."

Druga did not look at her more, but went in and sat at the board where the thousand dead stared, each stony eye broodingly centered upon the spot where he had placed Feronia. And as Druga's eye likewise centered upon that seat that had been the scene of a thousand deaths, he felt a wave of anger from the stony body of Feronia, and a sense of guilt came over him. He felt remorse that he should forget her and desire Eos. If he had known that those eyes were not dead, but seeing and remembering all that passed before them, he would have been shivering with fear of her anger. But Druga did not know. Yet it seemed to his senses that each of those eyes was likewise angry with him, and he got up in haste from that table of dead men and one dead woman, and went and drank wine by himself until sleep came.

With the first rays of morning light Eos woke him, and Druga learned that she had lowered the disk over the garden of live oaks beside the palace of Dionaea, and Druga looked out. No one was yet astir; they had not yet been seen. Druga and Eos descended by the ladder of ruby glass, and went side by side through the garden and Druga took the stairs he knew well up to the sleeping chamber of Dionaea. For in the many-locked cabinets of that chamber were her many acquisitions of magical apparatus, and if anything was there that would help them, they meant to find it.

As they entered the room, opening the door with a pick-lock, Eos cried out in a triumphant voice:

"We are not in vain. The Queen is not dead, Druga!"

The sleepy-eyed Dionaea poked her head above the covers at the sound of their entry. At sight of them, she hissed like a great snake, and writhed the long hideous body of Baena free of the encumbrance of the quilts, and Baena reared his own hideous, fanged head up beside Dionaea's.

Druga stood astonished to see the fabled Amphis-Baena here in the bed of Dionaea, and with the head of Dionaea! A great laugh broke from him to see the reptilian change the grafting had wrought in Dionaea's beauty.

Dionaea did not say anything, but Baena coiled swiftly on the bed and struck out full length, his fangs meeting in Druga's arm. Druga felt the terrible venom, like fire in his veins, and seized the great serpent-head in his two hands, squeezing in terrible anger. But Eos seized him.

"No, do not kill her! Carry her into the disk, and make her captive. I have conceived of a way of conquering Diana, and we need this creature alive."

Druga wrapped the great body around and around his body and arm, seizing the neck of Dionaea in one hand and the neck of Baena in the other. So burdened, he staggered down the steps and up again into the disk, and the trip took him a good hour, for Baena twisted loose and tried to flee, and he wrestled and fell from the ladder, and only succeeded by tying the writhing pillar of strength into a bow-knot and pulling it up into the ship with a rope.

Meanwhile the people of Armora had awakened from the tumult, and crowded everywhere about the gardens, getting underfoot and wondering loudly what this was all about. Eos hurried from the bedchamber of their Queen with a great bundle of material she had selected as of possible future use. They tried to stop her, but one glance of the potent magnetic power that flamed from her great eyes sent them all to their knees in worshipful, helpless adoration.

Druga, waiting above with the snake wound round with ropes and lashed to the pillars, watched this evidence of her powers with awe, for he had himself but narrowly escaped the swords of the guards, and had been about to plunge down the ladder with his own sword in a futile attempt to rescue Eos.

She sent the disk spinning upward in flight, and Druga took himself from her and went and sat by the writhing, fettered body of the Amphis-Baena, or Dionaea-Baena, or two-headed snake, saying to her as she spat venom at him:

"Listen to me, Dionaea, the best thing you can do for yourself is to try to win the favor of Eos. She is an enemy who has suffered as greatly as yourself from the work of Diana, and would help you if you earned it, to acquire a human body again. I think the snake himself would like that better too. He is too greatly married, I would say, to relish the state overmuch."

Baena relaxed at these words, and ceased to struggle. Then in great snake hisses, he made himself heard.

"Dionaea, I think too you should seize this opportunity to get out of this fix we are in. I gave you my tail to roost upon as a temporary measure, not as a permanent part of my future. Diana, whom we both serve, could have released us if she had been so inclined, and fixed us up with separate bodies, but she chose not."

That Dionaea was considering his words was evident. She ceased to spit at him, and composed her face into thought. Druga leaned back and smiled.

Eos brought the disk to rest again at the meadow at the foot of the glass bridge before Feronia's cliff palace, and came in to them. She stood gazing at the two-headed creature trussed to the pillars of the chamber. Feronia gazed at them with her stone eyes, and all the men gazed at Feronia as if transfixed by her stony beauty, and the sight made Dionaea shiver with apprehension. For she thought that these were people who had angered Eos and that Eos had changed them into stone. She wondered why Eos had added Feronia to the collection.

Chapter III

Eos sat beside Feronia and watched the great, writhing two-headed Dionaea, and waited. After a time the flowing golden bands of Life-energy entered, focusing subtly all about her, so that she seemed to Dionaea truly to be the Mother of All, and the greatest of All Goddesses anywhere.

At the entrance of the golden energy Eos smiled with relief, for now she had a power that she had not thought to use against Diana before. For to Eos this aversion to all men of the Goddess Diana spelled out the message of her weakness, and this energy of the life pole was going to pierce that weakness.

Day dragged after day, and the weird scene there in the banquet hall of the stone men of the past became to Druga a tense place of waiting for his own demise and change into a similar relic to decorate this hall of death. For Eos would not tell him what she planned for fear he would give her away in the tense moments that were to come when Diana at last rejoined her Dionaea in their strange dual existence.

The inducted energies of the female pole had a most disturbing effect upon the mingled male and female of the Amphis-Baena.

Baena, driven half mad by the increased female qualities of the head of Dionaea, made inadvertent love to her, caressing her face with his long forked tongue, and combing at her tangled hair with his fangs, always Baena was distraught with her attraction. This attention drove the woman near frantic, strained as she was in her unnatural condition, and she could not afford to anger the beast whose body she had been grafted upon. For even a serpent has been known to swallow its tail, and Dionaea had no desire to know if Baena could do that trick.

Eos, sitting quietly and watching the bound serpent, smiled at this continual by-play, and offered to release Dionaea for revealing her knowledge of Diana, so that some chink in her armor might be found. Not that Eos now needed any such thing, but she was kind-hearted, and wanted Baena at least on her side. For she could see into the dual life and thought of the two-headed monster, and knew that if Baena chose to set his will against Diana when she was within the body and mind of Dionaea – it would help her in what she planned.

"Baena," Eos at last said, "if you can find a way to help me against this unnatural mistress of your mistress, I will repay you by giving you anything you may ask of me."

Baena looked at Dionaea's head with the reptilian love-light glowing frustrate in his great green-and-gold eyes.

"If you will promise to give me what is in my mind that I desire, why then when the time comes I will see what I can do. I am weary of being the tail when I was meant to be the head, and if I had it to do over, this unnatural and self-willed appendage would remain in her proper place."

Now Eos knew that Baena could not help desiring Dionaea as a mate, for she seemed most reptilian in the strange snake-growth that had come over her, and knowingly she nodded at Baena, so that he knew that she knew what he wanted, but Dionaea did not know, for it never occurred to her. To Eos, what the future might bring to Dionaea as the mate of a snake seemed a proper revenge for what she had done in aiding Diana, and for other cruelties of which Druga had told her. She planned accordingly.

Came that day which was the time appointed by Diana Triformis for her visit to Dionaea. Much as she detested the need for entering the male body of Baena to interview Dionaea, still Dionaea had been a valuable ally, and Diana did intend in time to release her and give her again a human body.

To this end she had made some inquiries as to how this might be done. For in truth the method of doing so had evaded her mind in the excitement and rage of finding what had happened, and in the task of the spell she had created to turn Feronia into a stone image. For Diana knew that what Baena had accomplished she could accomplish, certainly, and the shame of forgetting how it might be done before the wise Baena's critical eyes made her neglect to mention her intentions to either of the two heads of the snake.

As the swirl of ethereal force that was Diana's traveling form settled within the golden-moted atmosphere of the great chamber of the disk-mansion, Eos stood up, and dropped from her body her insulating blue robe of shimmering magic, so that her supercharged beauty shone everywhere in blinding, awful attraction.

Druga, who had been sitting disconsolately talking to himself, rose to his feet like an automaton and walked toward that more than mortal beauty, his eyes blinded and his senses wholly submerged in ecstasy at the sight of the glory of Eos unveiled. As he reached the Goddess he put out his arms like a sleepwalker to take her to him, but she avoided him, seizing him by a wrist and turning him about, hissing in his ear, imperatively:

"Now prove to me that you are truly a mighty man of his word, with courage and strength, and in spite of this body of mine go out of this chamber and wait till I call without once letting your attention turn toward me or noting anything that goes on, else are we both lost!"

Like a man weighted down with lead on his feet, Druga strove to obey her, moving inch by slow inch away from that vast flood of energetic attraction.

Eos watched him move slowly away from her, every muscle standing out on his body and his neck corded with effort to keep his head turned away, and a vast admiration for him rose in her throat and choked her. It seemed to her that the statue of Feronia moved and that the stone face changed, suffused for an instant with admiration also.

The swirling purple cloud of Diana's entrance moved nearer to Dionaea, for in the hyper-space of her traveling, the points and dimensions of this world were much alike, and she did not realize that Dionaea was not in her palace at Armora. Settling about the two-headed creature lashed fast to the pillars of the chamber, she moved herself within the snake body and came to rest within the body of Baena, the snake.

Looking out of the dual heads of Dionaea and Baena now, Diana Triformis, who was no stranger to dual and triple existence even in the same body, saw with those four eyes the naked body of Eos, reflecting, emanating, giving off in vast floods the focused energies of the Pole of Female Life-energy, and those four eyes fastened hypnotized upon that glory, female beyond any other life in all space.

Eos moved closer and closer to the bound snake, murmuring soft words:

"Oh, Diana, wonderful one, long have I desired you, for I know your secret, that you are not female as your body seems, but male. So I have decided to have you for myself, for I am weary of men, and want only the boy Diana himself for my love, forever. Come to me, Diana, and dwell with me here at the pole of love, and never leave me. Can you not see that the enmity that has sprung up between us is the result of misunderstood love!"

Now Baena, seeing his opportunity, thrust his own male personality to the fore, trying to sway the intricate balance of sexes in the weird self of Diana – and with his mind and his eyes upon Eos, made himself to desire that infinite female attraction, which was not hard, so as to add that much weight to the attraction which even a God might not resist unless, as Druga had done, he turned his back upon it.

Diana could *not* turn her back, and the whole sudden surprise of finding herself not in the palace in Armora, but here in the halls of her erstwhile enemy, Eos of the Dawn-light, made her natural male attributes become dominant so that she desired Eos mightily.

Trapped thus by the circumstances, the lashed serpent body of Baena which insisted upon gazing steadily at the vast and overwhelming beauty of the unveiled body of Eos, and by the ignorance of Dionaea as to what was going on, by her own masculine nature into desiring this essence of all female attraction, Diana gazed upon Eos while the energies sent by Eos' skill coursed in greater and greater ecstacy through her.

So it was that Diana fell in love with Eos, as Eos desired, and with the Gods, love is an overmastering passion that may not be resisted.

Now Eos and the trapped spirit of Diana conversed together, and at the subtle words of Eos and the overmastering attraction, Diana swirled out of the body of Baena and settled engrossed about the glowing glory that was Eos. Inward she was drawn, and mated there in mysterious communion with the Goddess.

"If you but had a strong male body, Diana, we could live here forever in love and ecstasy. Why not return one of the stone men of the past into flesh again, become a man instead of half-woman as in the past – and so learn anew to live and love differently and gloriously. . . ."

Such were Eos' words, made potent by the golden glowing energies within her, swaying the bemused Diana to her will. And Diana, with Eos' hands, went to the wall cabinets and set out certain magical apparatus, brewing an antidote for the stony seizure she had sent to Eos' lovers in the past. This liquid she poured over the male of stone that Eos selected, and even as the stone man stirred and quickened into life again, her ethereal self whirled out of Eos and settled into the reanimated flesh of the man.

When he arose to his feet and spoke, it was Diana herself who spoke and not the man who had loved Eos long ago. What this desecration of her past love meant to Eos we shall not know, for she hid it beneath languishing glances and subtle swayings of her body, drawing Diana to her, wrapping her arms about the reanimated being, and walking with the new male Diana out of the room and so to her own chambers.

Druga, as Eos had foreseen, had been unable to contain his curiosity as to what was going on, and had at last peered from the hallway where he waited, just in time to see the purple swirl that was Diana settle into and seem to reanimate the ancient long-dead stone image.

The emotions natural to a man rose in him. He was not sure just what he was seeing, but jealousy rose in him like a flame, and his passion so steadfastly controlled and so rewarded by the fickle Eos made this jealousy into a terrible, red rage against her who had withheld herself from him only to give herself to her worst enemy in the form of a man.

Druga, overcome with this jealous rage, strode out into the banquet hall of dead men, took from the side of one of the dead men a great war-axe of bronze, and hefting it in his hand as if it were a trembling feather plume, strode after the two figures like the wrath of God.

As Eos reclined sensuously upon her couch in her sleeping chamber, and Diana in the man's body stretched beside her, bending back Eos' head and planting there a burning kiss, Druga entered, and standing over the pair like an outraged husband, shouted in a voice he was unable to make articulate.

"Of all contemptible females, you two are the most. . . ."

So saying, and mouthing his disgust with a tongue that frothed with rage, Druga seized the reanimated man with one hand by the shoulder and flung him half across the room, whirling up the axe to send it through him from curly head to gold-bossed sword belt.

Eos cried out in feigned fear and anguish, for she had expected this development, and it was but one phase of the weapon-array she planned to overcome the powers of Diana. For she knew Druga, and that he would be able to act in no other way if he observed what was going on.

But the body of the man was equipped with a sword of antique but sturdy length, and Diana had time to sweep this formidable weapon from its scabbard and turn aside the down plummeting axe, so that it struck a great shower of sparks from the strange golden metal of the floor.

Druga, his rage unabated, only swung the axe aloft again, parrying Diana's thrust with the haft of it, and then as she ducked his next blow, the great side of the weapon struck her alongside the head; stretching her senseless upon the floor.

Eos, on her feet, had not expected Druga so quickly to knock the goddess unconscious, and indeed the purple mist of her hyper-space body was already rising from the unconscious form on the floor as Eos threw herself to the wall where a switch hung open, and with her face a glory of triumph, thrust the great handle upward into place.

As the switch closed, a tiny black vortice spun suddenly into being in the center of the room, and within the black swirl was a tiny golden center. Swiftly the black vortice grew until Eos and Druga were pressed against the wall to avoid the clutch of the power of the whirlpool. The purple mist that was Diana was swept along as a whirlpool draws a straw, faster and faster, and a great scream came out of the blackness. Within, the center of the golden core seemed to give a triumphant laugh as the purple mingled there.

For a time Eos and Druga watched the swirling gold and purple sentience mingling and struggling at the center, and as the golden core shone stronger and stronger and at last overcame the purple swirling entity that was Diana, Eos pulled the switch again open, and the black vortice of space-force lessened and finally disappeared.

That intense whirlpool of black energy had taken Diana back with it into the terrible current of space. Diana would live – but only as a mote of defeated consciousness whirled along forever into the depths of space by forces too great to fight.

The man on the floor raised his head, sat up, rubbed the great lump left there by the flat of Druga's axe – and his eyes met the flaming attraction of Eos' eyes. With a bound he was at her side, gathering her up into his arms, crooning brokenly.

"How long I sat and watched your grief and envied the other men who came for their brief spell of life in Paradise before the black witchcraft of your enemy made them into stone. How long I pitied you, poor Eos! How many centuries have passed, and now a miracle! I am alive, and have you once again! No other ever shall take you from me. . . ."

Druga picked up the axe that lay disregarded on the floor.

"That may be what you wish, stranger, and though you are no enemy, if it is Eos you desire, you shall have her only over my dead body! Arm yourself, and prepare to die!"

The stranger eyed Druga scornfully. With a sudden gliding motion, he had passed from Eos' arms and seized the sword from the floor, was driving with it for Druga's throat. Druga got the axe in the way of the sword, but an axe, whatever antiquarians may say, was never the best tool against a smart swordsman; and this man knew his way with the weapon.

He drove Druga to the wall with swift darting movements of the blade, and Druga had no time to swing the unwieldy axe, but had to keep parrying the thrusts with the axe-haft, holding it between his hands like a quarterstaff. In moments his life blood would have been spilled on the floor had not Eos cried out:

"Hold, you brawling idiots, I am for neither of you! What do you think I have gone through all this for, to have you two whom I love kill each other? Now put up the weapons before I loose my own natural lightning and send you both into that doom you can only guess at!"

Druga peered at Eos, startled, and the reanimated statue pressed the blade to his throat, but Eos struck it up with her hand as he turned to peer at her too, and then Eos opened both her eyes quite wide upon them so that a weakness came upon them both, sending them to their knees in strange thralldom to the energies within her. So leaving them, Eos walked out of the chamber and to the great hall.

After a time, when their reeling senses returned, the two men followed the foot-steps that still sparkled where she had stepped, like flickering motes of golden dust outlining her prints upon the floor – followed the steps like men out of their wits, half staggering.

As they entered the hall, Eos was repeating the procedure so recently gone through by Diana, preparing a great cauldron of the fluid she had used to bring life again to the stone bodies. They leaned weakly against the wall, watching her as she poured the boiling, steaming liquid over one after another of the statues. The first figure so bathed was the body of Feronia.

She came out of the stony trance like a fury, blazing one indignant glance toward Eos, then turned the torrents of her wrath upon Druga.

"You philandering booby! I made you what you are and you repay me by running off from me in my greatest need and taking up with this – this –"

"She released you from your stony prison, Feronia!" Druga said hastily, fearing she would anger Eos with whatever word she thought of to describe her rival – and Feronia was clever enough to avoid saying what she was about to say, but went on with her abuse of Druga.

"Never mind what or who she is, it is you that has shown yourself the ingrate, for she owed me nothing. You couldn't go to Mors, Daughter of the Night, and get this thing properly taken care of at once, knowing she was friendly to me, no! You had to wander off on your old grey horse, never thinking of Mors, and get yourself wrapped up with the first woman that you come to, and wind your affections all around the planet in pursuit of her. You couldn't even remember me for one little month! You – you – oh, Druga!"

With which outburst her voice broke, and weeping and saying his name over and over Feronia went into his arms and wept there on his breast for a long time. And after her tears were stopped Druga knew that Feronia would never mention the affair again.

Druga held the dear form of his loved one close and let her weep, stroking the raven black hair, within him the soft well of affection for her filling and filling with all the memories of her dear, mad, competent, unpredictable, tyrannical ways. Over the curling sweep of her dear hair he watched Eos reviving one by one the dead loves of her past, and thought to himself that at least with Feronia he did not have all those rivals to contend with. The slight line across his throat where Eos' magic had stopped the sword of one rival from letting out his life reminded him too that with Eos as she was now, there would be no day pass that some of these warriors would not try to get rid of some of the rest. Druga decided that after all, Feronia loved him alone, while with Eos there was no knowing what rivals he would have.

Now Eos got a great snake out of the forest, a female, cunningly marked with little emerald markings, and striped with many colors, most venomous and snake-charming in its appearance.

This snake she quickly separated from its head, and placed upon its cunning female body the head of Dionaea, doing all that was needful successfully to incorporate the two into one life.

Baena's tail, which caused him great pain at the separation, she healed by applying a salve, assuring him that he would in time grow a new tail to take the place of the old, as is the way with snakes the world over.

When Dionaea awoke and found herself with a female snake's body, and Baena mooning over her like a lovesick coil of ship's hawser, she let out strings of oaths such as no ship's hawser had heard since the beginning of time. All of which seemed strikingly snake-charming to Baena, who only kissed Dionaea lovingly with his pointed tongue and assured her she would get used to him or he would devour her and seek a new mate elsewhere. With which assurance Dionaea ceased to curse and began to fawn upon Baena, saying:

"Why, how can you think it is your noble self I object to, Baena? It is just that I did not expect this development! I have grown so used to you that there is really very little difference, after all."

So conversing, the now lowly Dionaea and the now lordly Baena glided from the chamber and made their way down the ruby ladder of strange crystal, and out into the world. For it is only so that a male can leave the pole of the universal life force of the female principle, in the company of a female good enough to keep his mind from obeying the influence of the magnetic field.

Feronia, watching the scene, decided it was time for bed, and mentally taking Druga by the ear, led him out and down the ruby ladder and across the rainbow bridge of fragile glass into her own halls.

"Eos will handle her difficulties much the better without our presence, Druga. Besides we must get to bed, for in the morning there will be much work to attend to. . . ."

"What you have in mind?"

"Well, first we have to practice the magical performance we have just watched Eos go through, so that if we ever need it we too can release a figure from that stony curse of petrifaction. It is a most uncomfortable state. Then we have to return to Eos' disk palace and from her get certain information, such as the whirlpool she used to suck up the strength of Diana and cast it out into a current of force flowing through hyper-space – for we might need it sometime in the future."

"Which I devoutly pray you will not manage," murmured Druga, yawning. "I am too tired to even think about such a thing tonight."

With which words Druga stretched himself across the bed and straightway began to snore, and Feronia, who had expected a warmer welcome home than *that,* looked at him exasperated beyond measure. But then she insinuated her own witch's perceptions into his mind, looked over the somewhat shriveled memories of her that remained to him, and resolved to recreate his love entire before she strained it again with her impatience.

Outside, the great glowing magnetic field of female attraction pulsed and glowed and reached its strange streamers across the sky. The disk with its ancient, quaint, pillared and beautiful mansion, trembled in the current of the energy flow of the pole of life. In Feronia's hall a dark, small witch bent to her knees and prayed a prayer, with tears streaking her too-determined face, that this great sleeping man of hers would return his heart where it belonged.

Chapter IV

Now a witch's prayer is pretty apt to find its way to the God to which it is directed, especially when it is a white witch with black hair doing the praying, and not a black witch with white hair, as is so often the case.

Mother Mors, watching the small black-and-white-striped prayer winging its way across the deeps of night, reached out her hand and gathered it in to her whirling bosom, full of the milk of eternal kindness and soft with the vibrant softness of darkness itself, and read it there with the inner eyes of her heart.

That prayer contained some startling and incomplete information, and the mention of the passing of her enemy Diana whom she had tried to entrap herself for so long, brought Mors abruptly out of her sleep and sent her swiftly arrowing down upon the little valley where the golden pole now lit the whole sky.

The mystery and awesome power and majestic primal vitality of her silhouetted against and merged with the golden glory of the primal pole as the vast body of Mors merged and condensed and settled and came into human form there within the great banquet hall of Eos' palace on the disk.

Now as the body of the great Goddess of the night came into solidity before Eos, her laughter rang out, rich and ringing and with low, dark under-tones. Eos looked up from the great stack of ancient alchemic formulae where she sought the solution to the incredible quandary of too many lovers. For too-much-of-a-good-thing she could not find any reference in the books, for they were all designed to give only information on how to get rid of too-much-of-a-bad-thing.

Rosy to the tips of her fingers with embarrassment, Eos rose to her feet, her glory dimmed by the majesty of Mors' dark beauty, her height dwarfed by the tall, mysterious strength of Mors' indestructible figure, a figure such as must have caused the ancient artists deepest despair to depict in the least of its intense and vital and overwhelmingly sublime symmetry.

Mors' laughter made Eos blush till rosy was not the word for her.

"My dear Eos, can this be you? I would hardly have expected it of you, who have always been to me the personification of so many virtues. . . ."

"Oh, Mother Mors, I am glad to see you, in spite of this state of affairs – you can help me. You must know what has happened?"

"I can guess, but you had better explain from the beginning. Only a woman could know what to do here, it seems." Mors glanced around at the thousand and some virile males.

"You know the Pole is responsible for bringing them here, and one by one Diana turned them into stone as soon as my lonely heart turned to them for affection."

"It's a good story, but no one but me will ever believe it."

Eos only looked pitifully at Mors, and Mors took her to her dark, soft heart, and the vast strength of her poured into the vibrant soul of Eos, mingled there with that golden energy that made her what she was.

"Whatever I do is going to break their hearts – you know what this place does to men. I cannot love them all, but I *do,* and I cannot send them away empty-handed. You know what it *means* to them! It is really all that cruel Diana's fault!

"For ridding me of her I owe you a debt, and though you are but a child to my ages of life, I will help you avoid ruining the lives of all these fine men whom you have loved. Suppose I take them away with me, all but one, and give them back their own time and place before they found their way here – give them the will to want that life before they knew you, would that comfort you?"

"Only one?" murmured Eos, then blushed as she looked out over the thousand-and-odd faces that stared at her accusingly.

"Only one, and you must choose him carefully from among them all."

"That will take some thought," said Eos, her face full of indecision. "I loved each of them dearly."

Mors' face grew a little stern at that, and quickly Eos went on:

"I'll attend to it directly, Mother Mors."

"I have a little errand to attend to over at Feronia's, I will be back in a few beats of Druga's stricken heart. You could at least have kept your body hidden from him, out of respect for Feronia! I have not much patience with your dilemma. After all, there are other places to live, you know."

"But not for me, Mors. It follows me about!"

Mors' face grew even sterner, and Eos added:

"Of course I *know* that is because of the peculiar nature of the metal of which the disk is constructed, but *after all* you *know* it has been my home for so *very* long, I couldn't be expected to give up my home, could I?"

Mors only lifted one great dark eyebrow and lifted suddenly into dark whirling force and disappeared.

Eos, her face tear-streaked, went slowly down the endless line of men, examining each one carefully and cudgeling her memory to decide which one she had loved the *very* most. It was *so* difficult.

Mors, meanwhile, drifted into being over the sleeping Druga and the praying Feronia, still on her knees, her face upraised and very sweet with the dark-winged eyes closed, the long line of her throat sheer beauty in the dim light.

She touched the closed eyes softly with her potent fingertips, and Feronia opened them with a new understanding gifted into their structure. Then she softly entered Feronia's body and together they peered down into the body and the thought of the sleeping man, and with her dark fingertips vibrant with the energies of dark space, Mors went over each little nerve and passage in the brain where the energies of the disk and the Pole and the sight of the intense glory of Eros' body had burned out Feronia's years of love.

Everywhere she touched, a new awareness grew, centered and vitalized by the presence of Mors within the body of Feronia, so that nowhere was there any evidence of the loss of love, but only the beautiful memories of Feronia alive again within his mind, and wherever desire lived in him Mors touched her fingers, and planted a seed that would grow with good treatment into vital love. As she worked, Feronia wept shamelessly with thankfulness, and for every tiny node of love that Mors planted in Druga, one sprouted likewise in Feronia, and some of them were for Druga and some were natural gratitude to Mors for this work of replacement. The sleeping Druga stirred and his arms came about Feronia's hips where she stood by the bed. Mors sent her strange energies through the two lovers, marrying them there with the potent blessing that is actual magnetic mingling of being – and Feronia knew that only by abuse could she lose this man again!

"You are a good girl, Feronia, and you have a good man. I will visit you again, if that *Dark Master* wills it."

A chill went through the chamber at the mention of The Name, and Mors went out with the strange ecstatic sweep of entity, and Feronia knew what was meant by *God-head.*

Eos waited for a long time before Mors came again to her, for the God-head required certain things of Mors for this night's work.

As she at last reappeared to Eos, Eos did not note the terrific emotions of love-ecstasy upon her face, the record of her touching with *the One* upon the mention of him, and began to complain.

"How can I give them up, Mors?"

But Mors only looked at her with absent, flaming eyes, intent upon some far thing, and for the first time Eos noted the vast and subtle change in her, as if she had touched some vast fountain of beneficence somewhere in the while she had been gone. Her cheeks were flushed, her breast rising and falling. Mors was like a woman in love, or a Goddess touched by the love of Jove, and Eos' eyes fell before her sublimely, and only stood waiting for Mors to do what she must.

So Mors absently gathered up all the thousand-and-some men, tucking them into her bosom one by one, and whirled into the night with all but one.

As the Goddess Mors disappeared, a sudden suspicion struck Eos, and she whirled to look upon the man that was left behind.

She burst into tears.

The Red Dwarf reached out and patted her golden head. Then he stepped to the controls and sent the disk winging swiftly away.

"Where are you going?" asked Eos, lifting her head in surprise, and looking indignantly through her tears.

"To the opposite Pole of Energy, my sweet one," said the Red Dwarf. "Be patient a little while, and you will yet be supremely happy. Mother Mors is very wise. . . ."

And Eos was very happy. You see, I *do* know, for I was there. If it were not so, how could you be sure what I tell you is true? For it *is* true. . . .

The wise will understand what I have written.

www.ingramcontent.com/pod-product-compliance
Lightning Source LLC
Chambersburg PA
CBHW030416310726
48979CB00002B/431

* 9 7 8 1 4 6 3 8 9 9 1 5 8 *